This
Treasure Cove Story
belongs to

THE UGLY DUCKLING

A CENTUM BOOK 978-1-908497-89-5
Published in Great Britain by Centum Books Ltd.
This edition published 2021.

1 3 5 7 9 10 8 6 4 2

Centum Books Ltd, 20 Devon Square, Newton Abbot,
Devon, TQ12 2HR, UK.

www.centumbooksltd.co.uk | books@centumbooksltd.co.uk
CENTUM BOOKS Limited Reg.No. 07641486.

A CIP catalogue record for this book is available
from the British Library.

Printed in China.

centum

FSC
www.fsc.org

MIX
Paper from
responsible sources
FSC® C149078

A Treasure Cove Story

WALT DISNEY'S
THE
Ugly Duckling

By Annie North Bedford
Pictures by Walt Disney Studios
Adapted by Don MacLaughlin
from the motion picture *The Ugly Duckling*

One lovely summer afternoon, a mother
duck sat on her nest. In the nest, warm and
snug, were five beautiful eggs. The mother duck
sat very still, waiting for the eggs to hatch into
five little ducklings.

At last the mother gave a quack of joy and sprang off the nest. The eggs were rocking back and forth. From inside them came pecking and scratching sounds. The mother duck bent over to watch.

Then one, two, three, four eggs cracked open. And out tumbled four tiny ducklings, yellow as butter and soft as down, with bright eyes and cute little bills.

They all stood up and looked around. Then with soft little quacks they climbed out of the nest and waddled around in the shade.

What a beautiful family! the mother duck thought.

But then she looked at the nest and sadly
shook her head. For the fifth and biggest egg
had not hatched yet.

So she sat down again and waited some more.
Soon the big egg showed signs of life.

In a moment, two feet broke through the shell. Then a head appeared. But instead of being small and yellow and downy like the other ducklings, it was big and white and fuzzy.

'Honk!' said the new duckling, eager to be liked.

'Horrors!' said the mother duck. 'He doesn't sound like any child of mine.'

'Quack!' said the other ducklings. 'He's funny-looking, too. We don't want to play with an Ugly Duckling.'

And they waddled away with their mother.

The Ugly Duckling couldn't understand why everyone had left him alone. He followed the others down to the pond.

There he found the mother duck. She was swimming around the pond with the four little ducklings on her back.

The Ugly Duckling honked at them, hoping
for a ride. But the mother duck just scowled
at him and told him to go away.

Poor Ugly Duckling! There he sat, all alone at the edge of the pond.

Why won't they play with me? he wondered sadly. *Why do they call me ugly?* Big tears filled his eyes and trickled down to splash in the pond.

The Ugly Duckling, glancing down, saw
a strange sight. There was his own reflection,
all blurred and twisted with the ripples of the
water.

'Oh, dear!' cried the Ugly Duckling. 'I am
ugly indeed. I will run away and hide where
no one will see me.'

So he turned away from the sunny pond and
went slowly into the dark and gloomy forest.

How sad he felt there, alone in the forest, with
the silent shadows looming all around.

But after a while, he heard a friendly chirping. Baby birds were calling from their cosy nest.

They sound nice, thought the Ugly Duckling. *Maybe they will play with me.*

So he hopped and scrambled into the nest with them.

The baby birds liked him. 'And our mother will like you, too,' they promised.

The Ugly Duckling could hardly wait for the mother bird to come. Soon she came flying in with a big juicy worm in her beak. *Snap!* went the Ugly Duckling's hungry beak as he snatched up that whole big worm.

The mother bird was furious. She pulled
the worm away from him.

'Get out of here, you ugly thing!' she cried
as she chased the frightened Ugly Duckling
out of the nest.

The Ugly Duckling rushed to the pond as fast as he could go.

Everyone hates me because I'm ugly, he thought. Then he lay down on a log and cried.

'Honk! Honk! Honk! Honk!' The Ugly Duckling heard the sound over his crying. He blinked away his tears and shyly looked around.

There, right in front of him, paddling in the water, were four fuzzy white creatures just like him!

'What's the matter, crying on a beautiful day like this?' they asked. 'Come on in and play with us.'

The Ugly Duckling dived off the log and they all began to play. But in the midst of a lively game of water tag, his playmates suddenly swam away, honking happily.

The Ugly Duckling looked up and saw
– the most beautiful bird in the world.
'Mother! Mother!' his new friends cried.
'We've found a new little brother to play with.'

'Welcome home,' said the beautiful
snow-white swan, cradling the Ugly Duckling
in her wing. 'You are a fine, handsome baby
swan, and you'll someday be King of the Pond.'

From the shore, the mother duck and
her downy yellow babies watched the Ugly
Duckling's welcome.

'Come back and play with us!' they called.
But the little Ugly Duckling sailed happily
away with the swans.

Treasure Cove Stories

Please contact Centum Books
to receive the full list of titles in
the *Treasure Cove Stories* series.
books@centumbooksltd.co.uk

Book list may be subject to change. Not all titles are listed.